Virginia Woolf

Virginia Woolf was born Adeline Virginia Stephen in Kensington, London, England in 1882. Her father, Leslie Stephen, was a respected man of letters, and as a young girl Woolf was introduced to many literary figures, including Henry James. Woolf also made great use of the family home's vast library, working her way through much of the English literary canon as a teenager. Her summers were spent in St. Ives, Cornwall, which would later form the setting for her famous novel, To the Lighthouse.

In 1895, when Woolf was just thirteen, her mother died, triggering the first of her many mental breakdowns. Despite this, between 1897 and 1901 she was able to take courses in Greek, Latin, German and history at the Ladies' Department of King's College London. She even began publishing work with the Times Literary Supplement. However, in 1904, following the death of her father, Woolf suffered another breakdown which saw her briefly institutionalised.

Following her discharge, Woolf and her sisters moved from their family home to a new abode in Bloomsbury. It was here that Woolf met Lytton Strachey, John Maynard Keynes, E. M. Forster and various other writers and intellectuals, who together would form the famous Bloomsbury Set. In 1912, Woolf married author Leonard Woolf, who nursed her through another breakdown and suicide attempt. Woolf published her first novel, The Voyage Out, in 1915. This,

3

as well as various essays, quickly established her as a major public intellectual.

During the twenties, Woolf published the novels that established her as a leading figure of modernism and one of the greatest British novelists of the 20th century: Jacob's Room (1922), Mrs. Dalloway (1925), To the Lighthouse (1927) and Orlando (1928). Stylistically, Woolf experimented with a lyrical stream-of-consciousness narrative mode, and is now considered – along with fellow modernist James Joyce – one of the finest innovators in the English language. Her work has been translated into fifty languages, and her major novels have never been out of print.

After completing her last novel, Between the Acts, Woolf fell into a period of deep depression – exacerbated by the the onset of World War II and the destruction of her home during the Blitz. In 1941, fearing a total mental collapse, Woolf committed suicide. She was 59 years old.

Street Haunting:
A London Adventure

by

Virginia Woolf

Written in 1930

British Library Cataloguing-in-Publication Data
A catalogue record for this book is available from the
British Library

Street Haunting: A London Adventure

No one perhaps has ever felt passionately towards a lead pencil. But there are circumstances in which it can become supremely desirable to possess one; moments when we are set upon having an object, an excuse for walking half across London between tea and dinner. As the foxhunter hunts in order to preserve the breed of foxes, and the golfer plays in order that open spaces may be preserved from the builders, so when the desire comes upon us to go street rambling the pencil does for a pretext, and getting up we say: "Really I must buy a pencil," as if under cover of this excuse we could indulge safely in the greatest pleasure of town life in winter — rambling the streets of London.

The hour should be the evening and the season winter, for in winter the champagne brightness of the air and the sociability of the streets are grateful. We are not then taunted as in the summer by the longing for shade and solitude and sweet airs from the hayfields. The evening hour, too, gives us the irresponsibility which darkness and lamplight bestow. We are no longer quite ourselves. As we step out of the house on a fine evening between four and six, we shed the self our friends know us by and become part of that vast republican army of anonymous trampers, whose society is so agreeable after the solitude of one's own room. For there we sit surrounded by objects which perpetually express the oddity of our own temperaments and enforce the memories of our own experience. That bowl on the mantelpiece, for instance, was bought at Mantua on a windy day. We were leaving the shop when the sinister old woman plucked at our skirts and said she would find herself starving one of these days, but, "Take it!" she cried, and thrust the blue and white china bowl into our hands as if she never wanted to be reminded of her quixotic generosity. So, guiltily, but suspecting nevertheless how badly we had been fleeced, we carried it back to the little hotel where, in the middle of the night, the innkeeper quarrelled so violently with his wife that we all leant out into the courtyard to look, and saw the vines laced about among the pillars and the stars white in the sky. The moment was stabilized, stamped like a coin indelibly among a million that slipped by imperceptibly. There, too, was the melancholy Englishman, who rose among the coffee cups and the little iron tables and revealed the secrets of his soul — as travellers do. All this — Italy, the windy morning, the vines laced about the pillars, the Englishman and the secrets of his soul — rise up in a cloud from the china bowl on the mantelpiece. And there, as our eyes fall to the floor, is that brown stain on the carpet. Mr. Lloyd George made that. "The man's a devil!" said Mr. Cummings, putting the kettle down with which he was about to fill the teapot so that it burnt a brown ring on the carpet.

But when the door shuts on us, all that vanishes. The shell-like covering which our souls have excreted to house themselves, to make for themselves a shape distinct from others, is broken, and there is left of all these wrinkles and roughnesses a central oyster of perceptiveness, an enormous eye. How beautiful a street is in winter! It is at once revealed and obscured. Here vaguely one can trace symmetrical straight avenues of doors and windows; here under the lamps are floating islands of pale light through which pass quickly bright men and women, who, for all their poverty and shabbiness, wear a certain look of unreality, an air of triumph, as if they had given life the slip, so that life, deceived of her prey, blunders on without them. But, after all, we are only gliding smoothly on the surface. The eye is not a miner, not a diver, not a seeker after buried treasure. It floats us smoothly down a stream; resting, pausing, the brain sleeps perhaps as it looks.

How beautiful a London street is then, with its islands of light, and its long groves of darkness, and on one side of it perhaps some tree-sprinkled, grass-grown space where night is folding herself to sleep naturally and, as one passes the iron railing, one hears those little cracklings and stirrings of leaf and twig which seem to suppose the silence of fields all round them, an owl hooting, and far away the rattle of a train in the valley. But this is London, we are reminded; high among the bare trees are hung oblong frames of reddish yellow light — windows; there are points of brilliance burning steadily like low stars — lamps; this empty ground, which holds the country in it and its peace, is only a London square, set about by offices and houses where at this hour fierce lights burn over maps, over documents, over desks where clerks sit turning with wetted forefinger the files of endless correspondences; or more suffusedly the firelight wavers and the lamplight falls upon the privacy of some drawing-room, its easy chairs, its papers, its china, its inlaid table, and the figure of a woman, accurately measuring out the precise number of spoons of tea which —— She looks at the door as if she heard a ring downstairs and somebody asking, is she in?

But here we must stop peremptorily. We are in danger of digging deeper than the eye approves; we are impeding our passage down the smooth stream by catching at some branch or root. At any moment, the sleeping army may stir itself and wake in us a thousand violins and trumpets in response; the army of human beings may rouse itself and assert all its oddities and sufferings and sordidities. Let us dally a little longer, be content still with surfaces only — the glossy brilliance of the motor omnibuses; the carnal splendour of the butchers' shops with their yellow flanks and purple steaks; the blue and red bunches of flowers burning so bravely through the plate glass of the florists' windows.

For the eye has this strange property: it rests only on beauty; like a butterfly it seeks colour and basks in warmth. On a winter's night like this, when nature has been at pains to polish and preen herself, it brings back the prettiest trophies, breaks off little lumps of emerald and coral as if the whole earth were made of precious stone. The thing it cannot do (one is speaking of the average unprofessional eye) is to compose these trophies in such a way as to bring out the more obscure angles and relationships. Hence after a prolonged diet of this simple, sugary fare, of beauty pure and uncomposed, we become conscious of satiety. We halt at the door of the boot shop and make some little excuse, which has nothing to do with the real reason, for folding up the bright paraphernalia of the streets and withdrawing to some duskier chamber of the being where we may ask, as we raise our left foot obediently upon the stand: "What, then, is it like to be a dwarf?"

She came in escorted by two women who, being of normal size, looked like benevolent giants beside her. Smiling at the shop girls, they seemed to be disclaiming any lot in her deformity and assuring her of their protection. She wore the peevish yet apologetic expression usual on the faces of the deformed. She needed their kindness, yet she resented it. But when the shop girl had been summoned and the giantesses, smiling indulgently, had asked for shoes for "this lady" and the girl had pushed the little stand in front of her, the dwarf stuck her foot out with an impetuosity which seemed to claim all our attention. Look at that! Look at that! she seemed to demand of us all, as she thrust her foot out, for behold it was the shapely, perfectly proportioned foot of a well-grown woman. It was arched; it was aristocratic. Her whole manner changed as she looked at it resting on the stand. She looked soothed and satisfied. Her manner became full of self-confidence. She sent for shoe after shoe; she tried on pair after pair. She got up and pirouetted before a glass which reflected the foot only in yellow shoes, in fawn shoes, in shoes of lizard skin. She raised her little skirts and displayed her little legs. She was thinking that, after all, feet are the most important part of the whole person; women, she

9

said to herself, have been loved for their feet alone. Seeing nothing but her feet, she imagined perhaps that the rest of her body was of a piece with those beautiful feet. She was shabbily dressed, but she was ready to lavish any money upon her shoes. And as this was the only occasion upon which she was hot afraid of being looked at but positively craved attention, she was ready to use any device to prolong the choosing and fitting. Look at my feet, she seemed to be saying, as she took a step this way and then a step that way. The shop girl good-humouredly must have said something flattering, for suddenly her face lit up in ecstasy. But, after all, the giantesses, benevolent though they were, had their own affairs to see to; she must make up her mind; she must decide which to choose. At length, the pair was chosen and, as she walked out between her guardians, with the parcel swinging from her finger, the ecstasy faded, knowledge returned, the old peevishness, the old apology came back, and by the time she had reached the street again she had become a dwarf only.

But she had changed the mood; she had called into being an atmosphere which, as we followed her out into the street, seemed actually to create the humped, the twisted, the deformed. Two bearded men, brothers, apparently, stone-blind, supporting themselves by resting a hand on the head of a small boy between them, marched down the street. On they came with the unyielding yet tremulous tread of the blind, which seems to lend to their approach something of the terror and inevitability of the fate that has overtaken them. As they passed, holding straight on, the little convoy seemed to cleave asunder the passers-by with the momentum of its silence, its directness, its disaster. Indeed, the dwarf had started a hobbling grotesque dance to which everybody in the street now conformed: the stout lady tightly swathed in shiny sealskin; the feeble-minded boy sucking the silver knob of his stick; the old man squatted on a doorstep as if, suddenly overcome by the absurdity of the human spectacle, he had sat down to look at it — all joined in the hobble and tap of the dwarf's dance.

In what crevices and crannies, one might ask, did they lodge, this maimed company of the halt and the blind? Here, perhaps, in the top rooms of these narrow old houses between Holborn and Soho, where people have such queer names, and pursue so many curious trades, are gold beaters, accordion pleaters, cover buttons, or support life, with even greater fantasticality, upon a traffic in cups without saucers, china umbrella handles, and highly-coloured pictures of martyred saints. There they lodge, and it seems as if the lady in the sealskin jacket must find life tolerable, passing the time of day with the accordion pleater, or the man who covers buttons; life which is so fantastic cannot be altogether tragic. They do not grudge us, we are musing, our prosperity; when, suddenly, turning the corner, we come upon a bearded Jew, wild, hunger-bitten, glaring out of his misery; or pass the humped body of an old woman flung abandoned on the step of a public building with a cloak over her like the hasty covering thrown over a dead horse or donkey. At such sights

11

the nerves of the spine seem to stand erect; a sudden flare is brandished in our eyes; a question is asked which is never answered. Often enough these derelicts choose to lie not a stone's thrown from theatres, within hearing of barrel organs, almost, as night draws on, within touch of the sequined cloaks and bright legs of diners and dancers. They lie close to those shop windows where commerce offers to a world of old women laid on doorsteps, of blind men, of hobbling dwarfs, sofas which are supported by the gilt necks of proud swans; tables inlaid with baskets of many coloured fruit; sideboards paved with green marble the better to support the weight of boars' heads; and carpets so softened with age that their carnations have almost vanished in a pale green sea.

Passing, glimpsing, everything seems accidentally but miraculously sprinkled with beauty, as if the tide of trade which deposits its burden so punctually and prosaically upon the shores of Oxford Street had this night cast up nothing but treasure. With no thought of buying, the eye is sportive and generous; it creates; it adorns; it enhances. Standing out in the street, one may build up all the chambers of an imaginary house and furnish them at one's will with sofa, table, carpet. That rug will do for the hall. That alabaster bowl shall stand on a carved table in the window. Our merrymaking shall be reflected in that thick round mirror. But, having built and furnished the house, one is happily under no obligation to possess it; one can dismantle it in the twinkling of an eye, and build and furnish another house with other chairs and other glasses. Or let us indulge ourselves at the antique jewellers, among the trays of rings and the hanging necklaces. Let us choose those pearls, for example, and then imagine how, if we put them on, life would be changed. It becomes instantly between two and three in the morning; the lamps are burning very white in the deserted streets of Mayfair. Only motorcars are abroad at this hour, and one has a sense of emptiness, of airiness, of secluded gaiety. Wearing pearls, wearing silk, one steps out on to a balcony which overlooks the gardens of sleeping Mayfair. There are a few lights in the bedrooms of great peers returned from Court, of silk-stockinged footmen, of dowagers who have pressed the hands of statesmen. A cat creeps along the garden wall. Love-making is going on sibilantly, seductively in the darker places of the room behind thick green curtains. Strolling sedately as if he were promenading a terrace beneath which the shires and counties of England lie sun-bathed, the aged Prime Minister recounts to Lady So-and–So with the curls and the emeralds the true history of some great crisis in the affairs of the land. We seem to be riding on the top of the highest mast of the tallest ship; and yet at the same time we know that nothing of this sort matters; love is not proved thus, nor great achievements completed thus; so that we sport with the moment and preen our feathers in it lightly, as we stand on the balcony watching the moonlit cat creep along Princess Mary's garden wall.

But what could be more absurd? It is, in fact, on the stroke of six; it is a winter's evening; we are walking to the Strand to buy a pencil. How, then, are we also on a balcony, wearing pearls in June? What could be more absurd? Yet it is nature's

13

folly, not ours. When she set about her chief masterpiece, the making of man, she should have thought of one thing only. Instead, turning her head, looking over her shoulder, into each one of us she let creep instincts and desires which are utterly at variance with his main being, so that we are streaked, variegated, all of a mixture; the colours have run. Is the true self this which stands on the pavement in January, or that which bends over the balcony in June? Am I here, or am I there? Or is the true self neither this nor that, neither here nor there, but something so varied and wandering that it is only when we give the rein to its wishes and let it take its way unimpeded that we are indeed ourselves? Circumstances compel unity; for convenience sake a man must be a whole. The good citizen when he opens his door in the evening must be banker, golfer, husband, father; not a nomad wandering the desert, a mystic staring at the sky, a debauchee in the slums of San Francisco, a soldier heading a revolution, a pariah howling with scepticism and solitude. When he opens his door, he must run his fingers through his hair and put his umbrella in the stand like the rest.

But here, none too soon, are the second-hand bookshops. Here we find anchorage in these thwarting currents of being; here we balance ourselves after the splendours and miseries of the streets. The very sight of the bookseller's wife with her foot on the fender, sitting beside a good coal fire, screened from the door, is sobering and cheerful. She is never reading, or only the newspaper; her talk, when it leaves bookselling, which it does so gladly, is about hats; she likes a hat to be practical, she says, as well as pretty. 0 no, they don't live at the shop; they live in Brixton; she must have a bit of green to look at. In summer a jar of flowers grown in her own garden is stood on the top of some dusty pile to enliven the shop. Books are everywhere; and always the same sense of adventure fills us. Second-hand books are wild books, homeless books; they have come together in vast flocks of variegated feather, and have a charm which the domesticated volumes of the library lack. Besides, in this random miscellaneous company we may rub against some complete stranger who will, with luck, turn into the best friend we have in the world. There is always a hope, as we reach down some grayish-white book from an upper shelf, directed by its air of shabbiness and desertion, of meeting here with a man who set out on horseback over a hundred years ago to explore the woollen market in the Midlands and Wales; an unknown traveller, who stayed at inns, drank his pint, noted pretty girls and serious customs, wrote it all down stiffly, laboriously for sheer love of it (the book was published at his own expense); was infinitely prosy, busy, and matter-of-fact, and so let flow in without his knowing it the very scent of hollyhocks and the hay together with such a portrait of himself as gives him forever a seat in the warm corner of the mind's inglenook. One may buy him for eighteen pence now. He is marked three and sixpence, but the bookseller's wife, seeing how shabby the covers are and how long the book has stood there since it was bought at some sale of a gentleman's library in Suffolk, will let it go at that.

15

Thus, glancing round the bookshop, we make other such sudden capricious friendships with the unknown and the vanished whose only record is, for example, this little book of poems, so fairly printed, so finely engraved, too, with a portrait of the author. For he was a poet and drowned untimely, and his verse, mild as it is and formal and sententious, sends forth still a frail fluty sound like that of a piano organ played in some back street resignedly by an old Italian organ-grinder in a corduroy jacket. There are travellers, too, row upon row of them, still testifying, indomitable spinsters that they were, to the discomforts that they endured and the sunsets they admired in Greece when Queen Victoria was a girl. A tour in Cornwall with a visit to the tin mines was thought worthy of voluminous record. People went slowly up the Rhine and did portraits of each other in Indian ink, sitting reading on deck beside a coil of rope; they measured the pyramids; were lost to civilization for years; converted negroes in pestilential swamps. This packing up and going off, exploring deserts and catching fevers, settling in India for a lifetime, penetrating even to China and then returning to lead a parochial life at Edmonton, tumbles and tosses upon the dusty floor like an uneasy sea, so restless the English are, with the waves at their very door. The waters of travel and adventure seem to break upon little islands of serious effort and lifelong industry stood in jagged column upon the floor. In these piles of puce-bound volumes with gilt monograms on the back, thoughtful clergymen expound the gospels; scholars are to be heard with their hammers and their chisels chipping clear the ancient

16

texts of Euripides and Aeschylus. Thinking, annotating, expounding goes on at a prodigious rate all around us and over everything, like a punctual, everlasting tide, washes the ancient sea of fiction. Innumerable volumes tell how Arthur loved Laura and they were separated and they were unhappy and then they met and they were happy ever after, as was the way when Victoria ruled these islands.

The number of books in the world is infinite, and one is forced to glimpse and nod and move on after a moment of talk, a flash of understanding, as, in the street outside, one catches a word in passing and from a chance phrase fabricates a lifetime. It is about a woman called Kate that they are talking, how "I said to her quite straight last night ... if you don't think I'm worth a penny stamp, I said ..." But who Kate is, and to what crisis in their friendship that penny stamp refers, we shall never know; for Kate sinks under the warmth of their volubility; and here, at the street corner, another page of the volume of life is laid open by the sight of two men consulting under the lamp-post. They are spelling out the latest wire from Newmarket in the stop press news. Do they think, then, that fortune will ever convert their rags into fur and broadcloth, sling them with watch-chains, and plant diamond pins where there is now a ragged open shirt? But the main stream of walkers at this hour sweeps too fast to let us ask such questions. They are wrapt, in this short passage from work to home, in some narcotic dream, now that they are free from the desk, and have the fresh air on their cheeks. They put on those bright clothes which they must hang up and lock the key upon all the rest of the day, and are great cricketers, famous actresses, soldiers who have saved their country at the hour of need. Dreaming, gesticulating, often muttering a few words aloud, they sweep over the Strand and across Waterloo Bridge whence they will be slung in long rattling trains, to some prim little villa in Barnes or Surbiton where the sight of the clock in the hall and the smell of the supper in the basement puncture the dream.

But we are come to the Strand now, and as we hesitate on the curb, a little rod about the length of one's finger begins to lay its bar across the velocity and abundance of life. "Really I must — really I must"— that is it. Without investigating the demand, the mind cringes to the accustomed tyrant. One must, one always must, do something or other; it is not allowed one simply to enjoy oneself. Was it not for this reason that, some time ago, we fabricated the excuse, and invented the necessity of buying something? But what was it? Ah, we remember, it was a pencil. Let us go then and buy this pencil. But just as we are turning to obey the command, another self disputes the right of the tyrant to insist. The usual conflict comes about. Spread out behind the rod of duty we see the whole breadth of the river Thames — wide, mournful, peaceful. And we see it through the eyes of somebody who is leaning over the Embankment on a summer evening, without a care in the world. Let us put off buying the pencil; let us go in search of this person — and soon it becomes apparent that this person is ourselves. For if we could stand there where we stood six months ago, should we not be again as we were

18

then — calm, aloof, content? Let us try then. But the river is rougher and greyer than we remembered. The tide is running out to sea. It brings down with it a tug and two barges, whose load of straw is tightly bound down beneath tarpaulin covers. There is, too, close by us, a couple leaning over the balustrade with the curious lack of self-consciousness lovers have, as if the importance of the affair they are engaged on claims without question the indulgence of the human race. The sights we see and the sounds we hear now have none of the quality of the past; nor have we any share in the serenity of the person who, six months ago, stood precisely were we stand now. His is the happiness of death; ours the insecurity of life. He has no future; the future is even now invading our peace. It is only when we look at the past and take from it the element of uncertainty that we can enjoy perfect peace. As it is, we must turn, we must cross the Strand again, we must find a shop where, even at this hour, they will be ready to sell us a pencil.

It is always an adventure to enter a new room for the lives and characters of its owners have distilled their atmosphere into it, and directly we enter it we breast some new wave of emotion. Here, without a doubt, in the stationer's shop people had been quarrelling. Their anger shot through the air. They both stopped; the old woman — they were husband and wife evidently — retired to a back room; the old man whose rounded forehead and globular eyes would have looked well on the frontispiece of some Elizabethan folio, stayed to serve us. "A pencil, a pencil," he repeated, "certainly, certainly." He spoke with the distraction yet effusiveness of one whose emotions have been roused and checked in full flood. He began opening box after box and shutting them again. He said that it was very difficult to find things when they kept so many different articles. He launched into a story about some legal gentleman who had got into deep waters owing to the conduct of his wife. He had known him for years; he had been connected with the Temple for half a century, he said, as if he wished his wife in the back room to overhear him. He upset a box of rubber bands. At last, exasperated by his incompetence, he pushed the swing door open and called out roughly: "Where d'you keep the pencils?" as if his wife had hidden them. The old lady came in. Looking at nobody, she put her hand with a fine air of righteous severity upon the right box. There were pencils. How then could he do without her? Was she not indispensable to him? In order to keep them there, standing side by side in forced neutrality, one had to be particular in one's choice of pencils; this was too soft, that too hard. They stood silently looking on. The longer they stood there, the calmer they grew; their heat was going down, their anger disappearing. Now, without a word said on either side, the quarrel was made up. The old man, who would not have disgraced Ben Jonson's title-page, reached the box back to its proper place, bowed profoundly his good-night to us, and they disappeared. She would get out her sewing; he would read his newspaper; the canary would scatter them impartially with seed. The quarrel was over.

In these minutes in which a ghost has been sought for,

a quarrel composed, and a pencil bought, the streets had become completely empty. Life had withdrawn to the top floor, and lamps were lit. The pavement was dry and hard; the road was of hammered silver. Walking home through the desolation one could tell oneself the story of the dwarf, of the blind men, of the party in the Mayfair mansion, of the quarrel in the stationer's shop. Into each of these lives one could penetrate a little way, far enough to give oneself the illusion that one is not tethered to a single mind, but can put on briefly for a few minutes the bodies and minds of others. One could become a washerwoman, a publican, a street singer. And what greater delight and wonder can there be than to leave the straight lines of personality and deviate into those footpaths that lead beneath brambles and thick tree trunks into the heart of the forest where live those wild beasts, our fellow men?

That is true: to escape is the greatest of pleasures; street haunting in winter the greatest of adventures. Still as we approach our own doorstep again, it is comforting to feel the old possessions, the old prejudices, fold us round; and the self, which has been blown about at so many street corners, which has battered like a moth at the flame of so many inaccessible lanterns, sheltered and enclosed. Here again is the usual door; here the chair turned as we left it and the china bowl and the brown ring on the carpet. And here — let us examine it tenderly, let us touch it with reverence — is the only spoil we have retrieved from all the treasures of the city, a lead pencil.

Lightning Source UK Ltd.
Milton Keynes UK
UKOW02f1523280816

281633UK00001B/45/P